I0749203

FROGLAND

TAHIR SHAH

FROGLAND

A Teaching Story

TAHIR SHAH

MMXXIV

Secretum Mundi Publishing Ltd
124 City Road
London
EC1V 2NX
United Kingdom

www.secretum-mundi.com
info@secretum-mundi.com

First published by Secretum Mundi Publishing Ltd, 2024
A version of this story originally appeared in *Scorpion Soup*, by Tahir Shah, 2013.

FROGLAND

A CIP catalogue record for this title is available from the British Library.

ISBN 978-1-915876-02-7

VERSION 08042024

Visit the author's website:
Tahirshah.com

Drink the sourest water but imagine that it is sherbet.

Persian saying

Teaching Stories

When I was small, I was told stories from morning till night.

I was told stories about genies and witches and about great birds that could carry away elephants on their wings… and stories about distant kingdoms and magical lands ruled by warrior kings.

I was told stories of good and bad… stories of hope and others of despair.

I was even told stories about stories.

And all the while, I listened, amazed.

The more I listened, the more my mind worked… and the more I came to understand that these stories had a power about them, a secret lifeblood all of their own.

They were magical instruments, machineries that could alter states of mind and change the way we think.

But most importantly of all, stories can teach us, without us realizing that they are doing so at all.

Part of the default programming of man, stories are within us all.

Born into us, they make us who we are – they make us human.

Since earliest childhood, I have feasted on stories as a way of learning about the world, and learning about myself. They have been my dictionary and my encyclopaedia, my classroom, my guide, and my very best friend.

To descend down through the layers of stories is to be reborn, into a dominion of fantasy – one touched by real magic.

Pre-eminent within the great treasuries of tales, it is teaching stories like this one that have shown me the path to follow beyond the next horizon, and have made me the man I am.

Tahir Shah

Back in the days when the world
was inside out and upside down,
humans were slaves to frogs.

At this time, there lived in a distant land, twin brothers. As tall as he was handsome, the first was called Glorious, and the second – who was terribly short and odious to the eye – was named Grotesque.

To say there was sibling rivalry between the two would be the gravest understatement.

From dawn until dusk, Glorious and Grotesque bickered and fought, because Glorious did exactly as he was told and Grotesque always broke the rules.

Their squabbling began in the crib, continued through childhood and then into adolescence, when Grotesque's wrongdoing got them both into trouble.

And trouble came in the most severe form when the brothers attracted the attention of the frogs.

There was nothing frogs disliked more than humans who made a nuisance of themselves.

As rulers of the earth, the amphibians believed
that man had but one role to play –
serving them.

The frogs lived in vast, twisting labyrinths beneath the ground. They liked it there because it was damp and cool, and because it gave much misery to their human servants, whom they regarded as unclean and downright rude.

The frogs had presided for so long that neither they nor the people ever considered that things could be the other way around.

Generation after generation, the humans served the frogs, and the frogs amused themselves by tormenting mankind. They liked very much to point to the pale skin of the people, to screw up their faces and to hiss.

And they liked to empty Frogland's prison – where only humans were kept – and to take the inmates to the underground pool known as the Abyss, where they were thrown in and forced to swim with bound wrists until they drowned.

So it was that attracting the attention of the frogs was decidedly unwise… because the frogs never had a kind word to say to anyone who wasn't one of them.

On a damp, chill day, Glorious and Grotesque were brought before the Supreme Frog Council, their hands tied with twine.

The Great Frog Leader straightened his crown, licked the air, and croaked: 'I have it on good authority that you horrid humans have caused a disturbance to our brethren.'

'But Your Frogship,' said Glorious, 'we are twin brothers, of which there is one saintly one – *me* – and one immoral one – *him*. Ask anyone and they will tell you that there is the good and the bad.'

‘Silence!’ croaked the Great Frog Leader.
‘I will speak, and only I!’

Fearing for their lives,
the brothers remained silent.

The Great Frog Leader consulted with his Supreme Council and, a moment later, he gave judgment.

‘You are both to be cast into the Abyss,’ he said. ‘And nothing you can say or do will make us change our minds.’

Before they could protest, the twins were being prodded through the dank labyrinth towards the Abyss.

'It's all your fault,' Glorious snapped as they shuffled forwards, 'I've never done anything bad in my life!'

‘You’re so damned sanctimonious,’ retorted his brother, ‘what a tedious and virtuous life you’ve lived!’

Silenced by the frog commander, the brothers kept shuffling until they reached the Abyss.

The chamber in which it lay was danker and darker than any other, and had luminous lichens and moss covering the sheering stone walls.

Perched at the edge of the deep pool,
the Great Frog Leader ordered the brothers
to swim for as long as they could.

With that, they were pushed in.

A great deal of splashing followed, in which Glorious did exactly as he was told. He swam up and down, his legs kicking wildly.

Within a few minutes he had drowned.

Grotesque, on the other hand, disobeyed the orders. He was damned if a frog was going to tell him how to die.

So, taking the deepest breath of his life, he swam down towards the bottom of the pool.

As he swam, he found he could see quite
well. The deeper down he went, the more
oxygen there was in the water. So much so
that, right down on the floor of the pool,
he found that he could actually breathe.
By rasping his bindings on a jagged
rock, he managed to free his hands.

Glancing around, he noticed that in the darkest corner of the pool there was a narrow cleft. Grotesque swam over to it and, after a lot of wriggling, he managed to scrape through.

The passage twisted to the left, then the right,
doubled back on itself time and again,
but Grotesque kept going.

The thought of the frogs waiting up on the surface to cart away his corpse was reason enough not to give up.

Eventually, a long distance from the entrance of the cleft between the rocks, the surviving twin rose to the surface of a shallow pool.

Emerging into blinding sunlight,
he stepped from the clear water, dazed,
but thrilled to be alive.

Almost immediately he found himself surrounded by people.

But they were not ordinary people like him. Rather, they had human bodies with the heads of sheep.

‘*Baa, baa*! He has come!’
bleated one of the sheep.
‘You are right!’ chorused the others.

‘*Baa*! At last! After so many centuries, *baa*!’
cried another.
‘The scriptures did not lie!’
‘He’s so handsome!’ bleated the first.

Stepping onto the dry land, Grotesque took in the congregation of creatures huddling closer. He wondered if he were dreaming.

But before he could give it any thought,
the sheep-people carried him away.

The next thing he knew, the less-favoured twin was reclining in an immense alabaster palace, one that had been kept for centuries just for him.

Sheep-headed maidens doted on his every whim, feeding him choice morsels from platters of food. As they did so, they sang to him – the sacred ballad of the sheep-people.

Unable to believe his sudden reverse in fortunes, Grotesque congratulated himself on surviving, and on having become a deity to the misguided community of sheep-people.

Each day that passed, the maidens brought food more delicious than the day before, and insisted that he gorged himself more and more.

And each day, the kind of food that was brought was fattier and fattier – so that very soon Grotesque ballooned outwards in size.

When he refused to eat any more, the maidens fluttered their long sheepish lashes at him, giggling until he could resist no more.

Many days passed and Grotesque found he could hardly walk, so corpulent had he become. But, as the maidens reminded him, there was no need for him to take to his feet, because they were there to serve him – to fulfil his smallest whim.

Then, early one morning, the maidens came to Grotesque's chamber in a special procession. Some were playing lyres, others singing, all dancing.

‘This is a very special day, O Dearest One!’
they called in unison.

‘Not more food,’ the twin spluttered. ‘I just
can’t eat any more!’

'No, no,' said the chief maiden,
'there is nothing to eat. We're going
to bathe you instead.'

Leading the twin through into the royal bathroom, they washed him as he had never been washed before. After that, they adorned his body with perfumes and massaged him with rare oils.

'This is indeed a very special day,' gasped Grotesque. 'I do hope there'll be many more days like this to come.'

Strumming on their lyres, the morning air warmed by their voices, the maidens led their guest to the hillside beyond the village where the palace lay. Giggling and prancing about, they regarded him suggestively and giggled all the more.

As he wondered what was to happen next,
Grotesque was taken to a great slab of marble
sprinkled with rhododendron flowers,
and anointed with oil.

Before he could protest, he was tied down,
his wrists and ankles snapped into manacles.
'What's happening?!' yelled the surviving twin.
'What are you doing to me?'

The maidens tittered and laughed,
kissed him goodbye, and wandered away,
the lyres strumming as they went.
'Come back! Come back!' shouted Grotesque.

But the maidens did not turn.

Sunset came, and with the night came terrible cold.

Manacled and left to survive the elements,
Grotesque coaxed himself to do whatever
was not expected of him.

‘They expect me to collapse and die,’ he said to himself. ‘Well, I’ll be damned if that’s what I am going to do. I’m going to survive because that’s what I do best.’

Just as Grotesque was trying to work out how to free himself, a giant bird swooped down and began pecking at him. It soon became very clear that the bird was used to feeding on the white marble slab – which was an altar.

By twisting this way and that a few inches, Grotesque managed to angle the bird towards his wrists. A couple of pecks from the beak and his left hand became free. Moving fast, swinging his weight around, he freed his other hand, and then his ankles as well.

Rather than cowering on the ground as some might have done, Grotesque grabbed hold of the bird's tail feathers and clung on for his life.

The creature soared into the air.

Far below, Grotesque caught sight of the lines of sheep-headed people going about their daily work, and the palace where he had been fattened up before ending up as a sacrifice.

Despite the added weight of its payload, the bird reached a terrific height and flapped out to sea. Soaring higher and higher until the air grew thin, it crossed a vast expanse of water, and then a desert, with Grotesque holding on all the while.

From time to time, the great bird seemed to glance down, as if aware of its human passenger.

Nuzzling into the creature's plumage for warmth, the twin scanned the landscape below, desperately hoping he might be reunited gently with the earth.

All of a sudden, he spied a narrow ribbon of water bisecting olive-green fields in which farmers were toiling. Fingers straining to breaking point, he waited until he was directly above the canal…

… and he let go.

And fell…

Down.
Down.
Down.

Tumbling head over heels, he descended for what seemed an eternity, before the force of the fall was cushioned by a field of wheat.

As it happened, a procession was passing through the fields that day, a cortege of priests giving worship to the land. They were plodding in silence along the margin of the waterway when Grotesque tumbled from the sky.

Believing him to be a divine being, they hauled him to the riverbank, pulled him out, and garlanded him with flowers.

They called him Opee, which in their language meant 'heavenly', and they carried him to a mountaintop monastery where the gods were said to have lived since before time began.

Down in the village, the farmers and their families heard about Opee, and they all wanted to see him. But the clergy barred the doors and insisted that the Divine One was tired after his long descent from the clouds.

‘But we want to know all about him,’
said the people, speaking with one voice.
‘How dare you wish to disturb a divine being!’
snapped the head priest.

The farmers went off back to their fields, but
their minds were on the Divine One.
The head priest was thinking about him, too.

Having spent a little time with the stranger – a man with whom he shared no common language at all – he soon realized that the visitor's appearance was unpleasing to the eye. All warty and fat, Grotesque would surely have put fear into the people.

With time, the head priest came to see that he would be of much more use as a myth. After all, he might well have come as a scout for an invading army, or might even have been diseased.

A full week passed.

Then, one night, the farmers turned up at the mountaintop with pitchforks and fiery torches, and ordered the clergy to show them the man who had tumbled from the sky.

Fearing that he was about to lose control of the situation, the head priest slipped into the room where Grotesque was sleeping and he stabbed him cleanly through the heart.

Solemnly, he stepped out from the monastery and broke the news to the farmers and their families.

'I regret to inform you all that our beloved Opee has expired,' he said.

The farmers beat their chests,
while their wives and children howled.
'We want to see his body!'
demanded the growing crowd.

The head priest felt a pang of apprehension in his gut. Showing off the blood-drenched body – and such an ugly body – was the last thing he could do.

So he said:
'How dare you expect the body of a god
to be exhibited in death to mere mortals!
He must be buried in a grand funeral,
a devotion to the land in which we live.'

And so it was that Grotesque was given
a send-off more usually reserved for
potentates and kings.

Carved from jade, his coffin was rolled
through the streets in a special carriage
fashioned from silver and gold.

With every step, the community threw
flowers and pulled out their hair in remorse.

Some of the farmers went so far as to crawl
behind the hearse on hands and knees –
each of them chanting a single word
over and over:
'Opee! Opee! Opee!'

A master of showmanship, the head priest had a massive granite mausoleum constructed in the capital. The religious elite interred Grotesque and lit a sacred flame – which was to burn for eternity.

Day and night, a snaking line of ordinary folk wended its way up to the tomb, with pilgrims arriving from far and wide – all eager to pay their respects to the Divine One.

As the days went on, the head priest understood that more could be made of the mortal who had descended into their world. He devised a new faith called Opee around the Divine One's existence and, very soon, the new splinter religion had been embraced by much of the known world.

The numbers of converts surged into the millions and, as the power of the new faith increased, the head priest sat down to write *The Sacred Book of Opee*, a tool by which the myth of religion could be spread.

Finis

About the Author

Descended from a long line of storytellers, writers, and savants, Tahir Shah is one of the most prolific authors of his generation. He has published more than sixty books in numerous genres, including travel, fiction, and fantasy, as well as tales for children.

Raised in the tradition of Eastern 'teaching stories', Shah is passionate about stories and storytelling. He regards the ability to learn from folklore as being in us all, what he calls a 'default setting of humankind'. As well as having written scores of books, Shah has made documentaries for National Geographic TV and The History Channel. He is the founder and CEO of the charity, The Scheherazade Foundation.

Books By Tahir Shah

The Writer's Craft

The Reason to Write

Workbook: Comprehensive, Volume I & II

Workbook: Fantasy, Volume I & II

Workbook: Fiction, Volume I & II

Workbook: Historical Fiction, Volume I & II

Workbook: Teaching Stories, Volume I & II

Workbook: Travel, Volume I & II

Novels

Jinn Hunter: Book One – The Prism

Jinn Hunter: Book Two – The Jinnslayer

Jinn Hunter: Book Three – The Perplexity

Hannibal Fogg and the Supreme Secret of Man

Casablanca Blues

Eye Spy

Godman

Paris Syndrome

Timbuctoo

Midas

Zigzagzone

Nasrudin

Travels With Nasrudin

The Misadventures of the Mystifying Nasrudin

The Peregrinations of the Perplexing Nasrudin

The Voyages and Vicissitudes of Nasrudin

Nasrudin in the Land of Fools

Travel

Trail of Feathers

Travels With Myself

Beyond the Devil's Teeth

In Search of King Solomon's Mines

House of the Tiger King

In Arabian Nights

The Caliph's House

Sorcerer's Apprentice

Journey Through Namibia

Teaching Stories

The Arabian Nights Adventures

Scorpion Soup

Tales Told to a Melon

The Afghan Notebook

Daydreams of an Octopus & Other Stories

The Caravanserai Stories

Ghoul Brothers

Hourglass

Imaginist

Jinn's Treasure

Jinnlore

Mellified Man

Skeleton Island

Wellspring

When the Sun Forgot to Rise

Outrunning the Reaper

The Cap of Invisibility

On Backgammon Time

The Wondrous Seed

The Paradise Tree
Mouse House
The Hoopoe's Flight
The Old Wind
A Treasury of Tales
The Tale of Double Six
The Forgotten Game
King of the Jinns
The Destiny Ring
Changing the World
Cat, Mouse
Frogland
Mittle-Mittle
Capilongo
The Princess of Zilzilam
The Singing Serpents
The Tale of the Rusty Nail
The Unicorn's Tear
The Clockmaker Who Travelled Through Time
The Fish's Dream
The Man Whose Arms Grew Branches
The Most Foolish of Men
The Shop That Sold Truth
Qwerty
Renaissance
The Man With the Tiger's Head
The Kingdom of Blink
The Wisdom of Celestine
Dream Soup
The Skeleton Factory
An Unexpected Gift

The Problem Exchange
The Pharaoh Code
The Monkey Puzzle Club
Liquid Time
Cat Dog, Dog Cat
Princess Pickle's Laugh

Anthologies

The Anthologies: Africa
The Anthologies: Ceremony
The Anthologies: Childhood
The Anthologies: City
The Anthologies: Danger
The Anthologies: East
The Anthologies: Expedition
The Anthologies: Frontier
The Anthologies: Hinterland
The Anthologies: India
The Anthologies: Jinns
The Anthologies: Jungle
The Anthologies: Magic
The Anthologies: Morocco
The Anthologies: Nasrudin
The Anthologies: People
The Anthologies: Quest
The Anthologies: South
The Anthologies: Taboo
The Anthologies: Teaching Stories
The Clockmaker's Box
The Tahir Shah Fiction Reader
The Tahir Shah Travel Reader

Research

Cultural Research

The Middle East Bedside Book

Three Essays

Edited by

Congress With a Crocodile

A Son of a Son, Volume I

A Son of a Son, Volume II

Screenplays

Casablanca Blues: The Screenplay

Timbuctoo: The Screenplay

A REQUEST

If you enjoyed this book, please review it on your favourite online retailer or review website.

Reviews are an author's best friend.

To stay in touch with Tahir Shah, and to hear about his upcoming releases before anyone else, please sign up for his mailing list:

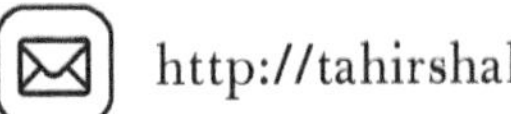

http://tahirshah.com/newsletter

And to follow him on social media, please go to any of the following links:

http://www.twitter.com/humanstew

@tahirshah999

http://www.facebook.com/TahirShahAuthor

http://www.youtube.com/user/tahirshah999

http://www.pinterest.com/tahirshah

https://www.goodreads.com/tahirshahauthor

http://www.tahirshah.com

www.ingramcontent.com/pod-product-compliance
Lightning Source LLC
Chambersburg PA
CBHW030522310726
48979CB00010B/1763/J

* 9 7 8 1 9 1 5 8 7 6 0 2 7 *